for all those who love fairy tales
and wish there were more
of them in the world...

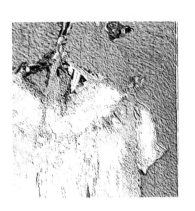

T. S. Poetry Press
New York
tspoetry.com

ISBN 978-1-943120-20-8

Library of Congress Control Number: 2018900007

Juvenile Fiction / Fairy Tales & Folklore / General
        The Golden Dress: A Fairy Tale for Children & Children at Heart
        Author, L.L. Barkat
        Illustrator, Gail Nadeau

Summary: Exquisite painted photography, digital art, and collage brings to life the story of a seamstress who gives her only daughter a golden dress that grants the girl's every wish throughout the years. But when the dress begins to age, the girl struggles to embrace the change—and risks losing her mother's heart and her own special place in the world. A blue lace wind shares the secret of what will be lost, unless the girl can find a way to open her heart and her hands before the dress completely disappears.

Companion materials available at **tweetspeakpoetry.com/literacyextras**

The Golden Dress

a fairy tale for children
& children at heart

by l. l. barkat

illustrated by gail nadeau

ts ♥ *literacy starts with love*

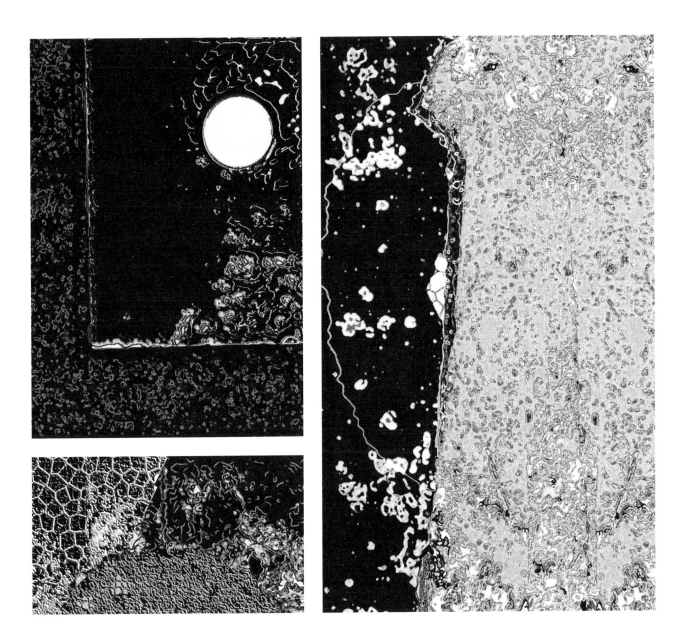

*T*here once was a dress. One dress.

When it was new, it was gold and sparkly and shimmery like the glow of certain stars on the darkest night.

It was made by a graceful old woman, whose fingers were as lissome as a ruby-throated hummingbird, and though she sewed quickly, she sewed with care, threading the dress with a hundred silken stitches along every inch of its beautiful seams and hem.

No one knew she had also tucked a small rosy part of her heart into the dress, because every seamstress keeps at least one secret, and that was hers.

*N*ow, like all things made with gold and a little part of someone's heart, the dress had a touch of magic in it.

So when the old woman gave the golden dress to her only daughter, it should be no surprise that whatever the girl wished the dress to be, it was.

When the girl was young, she often wished the dress would be painted red and white, like the big-top tent of a circus. A blue balloon should come along! And so it was. Complete with blue balloon.

When the girl outgrew the circus (or thought she did),
she wished the dress to be be painted in the wild colors
of jewels, and so it was.

The years went by in sapphire, jasmine, ruby, amethyst.
And though the girl could not see the golden dress's secret,
that did not matter. For it always held a small rosy part of the
old woman's heart, whether it was in its golden form or not.

*T*ime passed, and the dress became many things for the girl, who—in truth—was no longer a girl, but a woman making her way in the world.

The dress was painted fancy pearl for parties (and sometimes a lacy fan would come along!). The dress was painted crisp black, with a tell-tale golden edging, for wearing to important meetings. For the autumn fairs (which she never outgrew), the dress was painted pumpkin orange.

And still, though the girl did not know it, the dress always held a small rosy part of the old woman's heart, no matter what color or style it was painted, according to the girl's desires.

*N*ow it happened, as happens with all the garments we wear over time, that the dress began to show its age. (Not even magic can stop that, sad to say.)

The seams pulled, the colors muted, the gold began to fall away.

*S*ometimes, if the girl was lucky, the dress would look as if it would last forever. This is exactly how it seemed on the day that she wished the dress to grant her emerald.

But on that day, where in the past the dress would lavish a balloon or a fan or even sapphire roses to come along, a raven was in their place.

"It is time," said the raven.

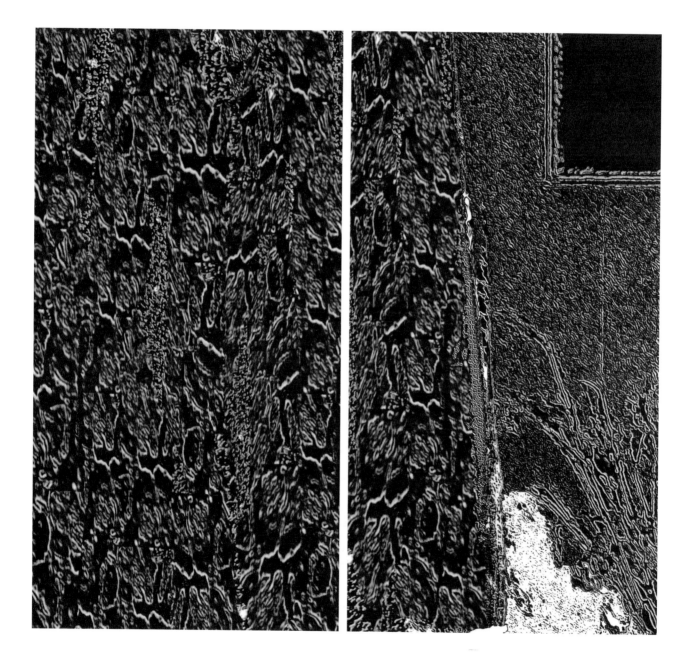

And the girl knew exactly what the raven meant. But she refused. She would *make* the dress do its magic. And everything would still be hers, in just the way she'd always wished it to be.

Enough with the emerald! It had brought the raven. She held the dress at arms' length and shook it, harder than an old dress should ever be shaken. "I want ruby!" she cried.

And so it was. But, if truth be told, the ruby looked more like the crimson of blood. And an arrow pierced its cloth.

The girl, never having learned that the dress contained a small rosy part of the old woman's heart, did not see the meaning of the rending. She was simply angry that the dress was most certainly unwearable with an arrow near its heart.

"You stupid old dress!" she cried. And in a fit of selfish wishing, she wished one wish after another, in rapidfire. The dress tried, as it always had. It strained. It bent. It pulled. No colors came. Not even the telltale edge of gold. Only the black of night, and a blue lace wind that whispered a secret to the girl.

"If you refuse, you will lose your mother's heart. You will lose the gold. You will lose whatever shred of magic still lingers in the dress's seams."

*S*he thought about this. She thought and she thought and she thought, but she could not bring herself to heed the raven's words and the words of the blue lace wind.

Days went by, then the days turned into years, and still she thought. Or so she pretended.

Until one day, when she looked to the dress, it had almost disappeared.

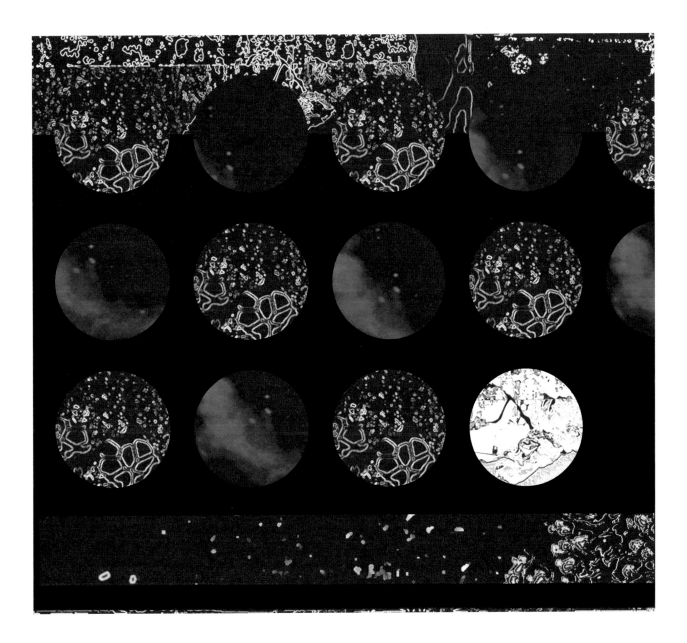

The room where it hung was white. The golden rod that it hung upon was also white. The dress itself was brittle white, with not a hint of rosy color. And in that moment, she understood.

A lump rose in her throat. A sorrowful emptiness knocked at the walls of her heart. A panic spread like wild horses, under her skin and to the tip of every finger and to the top of every toe.

The girl opened her mouth, but no words came. The dress seemed to shiver and fade.

She closed her eyes and remembered her mother's graceful hands, stitching the seams, stitching the hem. "I am so very sorry," she said to the dress. "I am so very, very sorry."

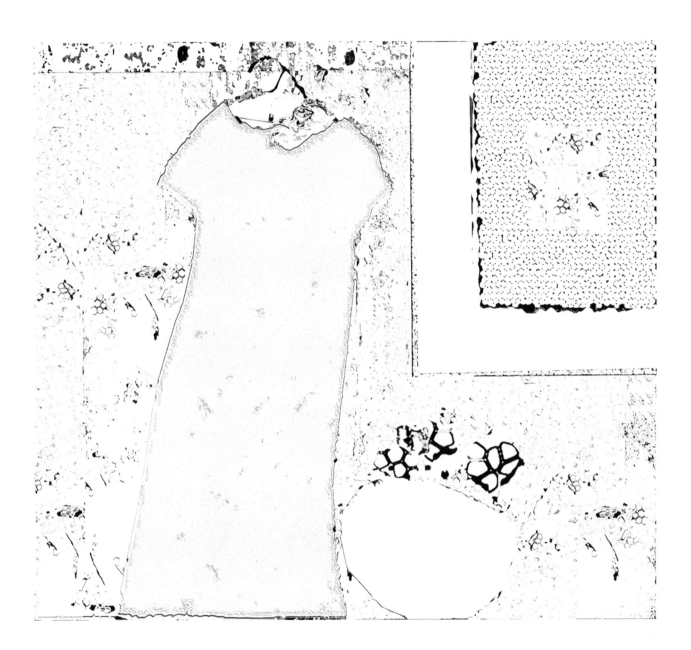

The dress began to shimmer and shift, and a cooing sound arose from its deepest fibers. "Open your hands," the fibers seemed to sing. "Open your hands, and your heart."

The girl (who was now a woman, more truly so than she'd ever been), opened her hands, and her heart.

Then a sound of flight filled the room of white. And the one dress, in a burst of magic, became a hundred colorful dresses for her to give away, to whoever she wished.

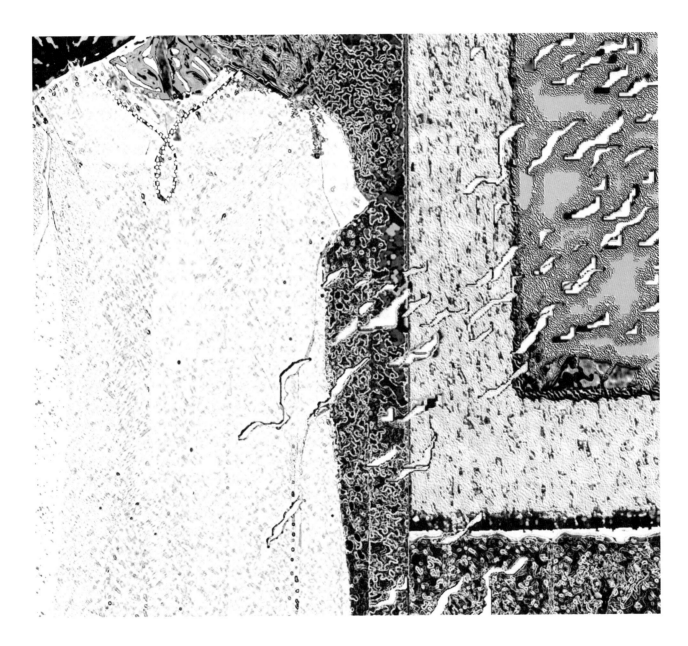

And that she did.

And every dress contained a small rosy part of her mother's heart—and a hint of magic in the seams.

About the Author

L.L. (Laura) Barkat has served as a books, parenting, and education contributor at *The Huffington Post* blog and is a freelance writer for *Edutopia*, as well as the author of six books for grown-ups. She's also the author of a new learn-to-read series and the beautiful *A Is for Azure: The Alphabet in Colors*. If she had a golden dress, she would wish for a pair of golden shoes to go with it. And earrings with rubies.

About the Illustrator

Gail Nadeau has been a fine artist for nearly forty years, and her house is filled with jewel-like colors and many, many pieces of art, including acclaimed works from series like *100 Angels*; *Black Velvet, White Velvet*; and *Doll House*. From a single surviving photograph of a lost family heirloom white dress, she has — through digital media, painting, and collage — created hundreds of pieces of colorful dress art, just a handful of which are featured here in *The Golden Dress*.

About the Publisher

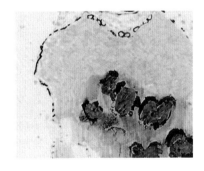

T. S. Poetry Press is the sponsor of **tweetspeakpoetry.com**, where whimsy and color abounds — around the topics of poetry, writing, and lifelong literacy growth. The Press promotes "poetry for life" and "literacy for life" through free teaching and learning resources, books for grown-ups, and books for children. The publisher is committed to cultivating literacy as one way to create stronger connections across the generations — with themes and co-learning materials that bring together grandparents and grandchildren, parents and children, and teachers and their students.

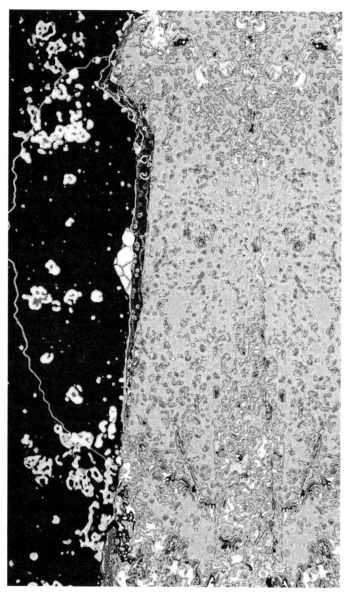

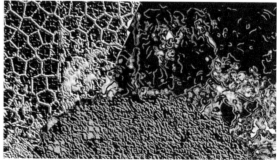

Proof

Made in the USA
Columbia, SC
07 February 2018